ELECTROID
THE SPARKY HERO

Harshit Agrawal

Invincible Publishers

First published in India in 2017 by
Invincible Publishers

ISBN: 978-93-86148-49-0

Invincible Publishers
G-120, Sushant Lok III, Sector 57, Gurgaon-122001

Opposite Kasturba Ashram, Radaur Distt
Yamuna Nagar, Haryana- 135133

Digitally Printed at Replika Press Pvt. Ltd.

Chapter sparky ball

* * *

"Yuletide". On this day, the Yard family had given birth to a charming boy in Bellwood city. After the birth of the baby (named Sam) hardly after two minutes, a meteor piece struck the floor of the earth in the Bellwood jungle. Sam's dad, James Yard was a renowned scientist in the country. James got a phone call that he had to hurry and come to the Bellwood jungle with his team for the research of the unknown meteor fallen there. James had to leave her wife July, and this son Sam to go on the duty which was important because James was interested in meteor and their research. When James and this team reached the place where the meteor was stricken, they saw lakhs of trees were on fire and destroyed by the meteor. The meteor rock was blue in colour and shining like a flash of a phone. The meteor was carried and loaded onto the truck to go to James' lab. When the meteor was loaded in the truck, they notices that the place where it ad fallen, got a pattern which was very much typical and could not be understood by the scientists. And some lady was also present there. There was too much confusion after seeing this pattern. Meteor was carried to James' lab which was mention as the world best research lab. The rock passed its first test by the diamond blade cutter. The edge of the cutter broke into two halves. The cutter which broke was the world's second best known cutter. Now James' effort was to carry out the second test. It was the laser of radioactive element Rutherfordium. The laser equipment was fixed at all the corners of the room were the rock was kept. James and his co-scientist activated the laser machine. The laser beam from all four corners struck the meteor. But suddenly the meteor rock started generating electricity and fired to the all corners. Later the machine resembled a bomb destroys the foe in the war. All the attempt of James and his team had failed. Only the last attempt they wanted to do was that of bombarding of radioactive elements on the rock. The machine was setup and James' team set up all the things carefully because they did not want to fail this time. Firstly they used Dubnium for their experiment. This unstable Dubnium proton bombarded the rock. James saw some behaviour in the rock but the Dubnium element finished and the experiment had to be stopped. Then the team used Seaborgium element which was more reactive than Dubnium element. The process was again started and they could see the behaviour of electron in the rock. And the bond was breaking slowly. This experiment went on for three years by different elements like Bohrium, Roentgenium, Copernicuim, Darmstadtium, Meitnerium, Hassnium and many more radioactive elements. James found that it was 6-D and now its bonding had lost but in these three years the workers who worked with James had left their job.

James put the rock in the collar of a boiler machine, whose reading read in kelvin. Firstly he started boiling it on 400 kelvin but nothing happen. Then he raised the temperature to 900 kelvin then its part started vapoursing. Then he again further raised to 2000 kelvin and then the whole rock disappeared then he decreased it to 10 kelvin. Then after some time after some blue light started appearing. He again decreased it to 0 kelvin then he saw a blue colour ball which was appeared in the cooler and the boiler machine. It was like a ball with electricity and named it "sparky ball" (which was sparkling in blue colour). Then he researched further more and got further information that it was a ball which created electricity by itself and any one who touched this ball their chest, this ball would break down and get absorbed by the skin. It then goes inside the heart to the blood and attaches to the RBCs. When large no. of electric shock get by the person who has absorb this sparky ball then only the power will be activated and the person will be creating electricity by it self. If a person encounters with high electric current, only then will the sparky ball get activated.

Far far away, around the Sun, a part of Sun fell. The was noticed by Dorgun. He thought that he would absorb this energy and would rule the whole universe by his power. Dorgun opened his tech. Hologram and started searching from where his lofty type of energy was coming. He got the reading from Bellwood, which is in America which was on planet Earth. Dorgun started his trip to planet Earth.

When Dorgun reached the exosphere of the planet earth, James got the information that some foreign body from outside of the earth had come towards his lab. His satellite also told him that the foreign body would be reaching in 5 minutes. James also knew that the foreign body was coming for this sparky ball. He wore the gloves and carried the sparky ball to his new invention, which was teleportal. He just started the teleportal and set the place (at his home) and pressed the start button. The teleportal started working and opened the gate. James walked with the sparky ball inside the teleportal. He walked two steps then he saw a dark room. It was his little three years baby Sam's room. Then James pulled the clothes of Sam up and touches the sparky ball at the place of heart. The sparky ball broke and got absorbed by the skin of his son Sam. James spoke "My son, you will be the guardian of this country and save this power from the dark evils. I will be with you forever and will bless you in all your endeavors". After speaking, he went back to his lab by the teleportal machine.

The satellite told that the foreign body would be reaching in 10 seconds. "10… 9… 8… 7… 6… 5… 4… 3… 2… 1". Some thing came from firmament and struck the roof of James' lab.

The foreign body was looked like a human being but looked rather dangerous. His eyes was burning like a fire and felt like the sun has come to his lab. "Who are you? Why have you come here?" asked James. "I am Dorgun, the part of Sun. Where is the power ball which you have created" asked Dorgun. "I don't know which power ball you are talking about" told James. "You are not afraid of dying" said Dorgun. "No. I will not tell you about the sparky ball. You can kill me if you please." told James bravely. "You are a very brave person. But I will kill you look for the rock without your help" said Dorgun.

Dorgun used this power of fire and put James into the flame of Sun. Within second James died. His body looked like a turkey that had fired in the hot oil of lava.

And Dorgun returned back to his home. There he used his tech. hologram for looking for the source of the power but no clue was found. "Oh! Such a stupid person I am. I have to wait till the sparky ball is activated and then only I will be able to get to know the source of the that power" said Dorgun.

Dorgun had read the computer of James before leaving the earth. The information was that if the sparky ball touches the heart. It would then be absorb by the skin and move through the RBC. "I still have to find in which human the call is absorbed." said Dorgun.

In the morning the news was aired that the world's best scientist James Yard had been killed in his lab. His body was burnt till death.

All the Bellwood residents reached the graveyard where the coffin of James' was going to be buried.

James' wife July was in tears and

said "James you were a great scientist. Our small boy Sam will be like you".

The coffin of James' was buried inside the earth. And all the people of Bellwood returned back to their home.

July and his son Sam also return back to there home.

"Mom, has dad died?" asked Sam.

"No my son, he has gone to heaven" told July.

Chapter After 15 years

❄ ❄ ❄

After 15 years Sam become a smart, mature, and a strong young boy. Now he was studying in Bellwood University Of Mechanical Science. Sam also wanted to become a scientist like his dad, James Yard. He made some mistake while working on some project. The electricity of that rock got absorb by the body of Sam in the form of a strong shock. It looked like Sam would be die after the shock.

At that time, the morning sun was at the head. The alarm rang 'Tee… Tee…' Sam was floating above the bed. He stopped the alarm and saw that he was above the bed. He tried to put does his leg and suddenly he fell on the bed and got hurt on his back. He was surprised that by the shock he got, was not low but rather very strong and he yet survived. Suddenly July called from downstairs "Sam come down for breakfast and then you have to get ready to go to your university". Sam moved downstairs to the garage and saw that the things were actually disturbed. The shock he got was not the dream. He was getting late to the university and forgot to see that it was a dream and moved to go for the university.

Due to the mighty shock that Sam had received, the sparky ball got activated.. Far away Dorgun felt the same energy and could know that it was the sparky ball that created it. He opened the Tech. Hologram and saw it comes from Bellwood city of planet Earth.

Dorgun sent his lakhs of men to bring that boy to him.

Sam was in the university. And the bell for lunch break rang. After Sam finished his lunch, he moved to wash room. Suddenly, outside the university many men came and took over the University. One faculty of that university tried to be smart due to which the men burnt him to ashes. All the students and teacher felt bad for the teacher who was tortured like that. Students and teacher knelt-down and they were all silent in the canteen.

Sam got a feeling that he was soon going to become a hero.

The men of Dorgun reached the washroom after finding the source of the energy were Sam was already present. Sam was washing his hand, when suddenly four men caught him tightly from behind. They all said "we will take you to our lord Dorgun who has told to bring you to him". They held Sam so tightly that he could feel the pain building up in him. Sam bowed his head and closed his eyes. Suddenly an electric shock came from Sam's body and struck the men. And when Sam opened his eyes, he saw the men had died and couldn't understand how it all had happen. He again closed his eyes and started thinking about what happened at that time, again electric shock came from Sam's body and struck the LED lights. The wash room was dark know. Sam rubbed his two fingers and separated it in a distance and saw some electricity coming from his one finger and went inside the other finger. Then he knew that electricity was generating inside his body. He pulled out the jacket of man and move the jacket in the opposite direction and wore it and took out his handkerchief and placed it over his face and did his hair is a stylish manner using water to stiffen the hair.

Sam moved to the canteen where everyone was present. Sam saw that one man had hijacked the university. He put his hand in the drinking water tank. As a man was passing the water tank, Sam rubbed his finger and silently touched the head of man by his finger. The electric shock passed from the head of the man and within a second, the man died. Like this he made 20 men of Dorgun fall into the hands of death. When Sam reach the canteen, he tried to keep out of sight and saw that lakhs of men. Then Sam saw an iron rod above the canteen. "Sam thought that he struck an electric shock to the iron rod then the electric shock would be distributed into many fragments and moved to the men who has hijacked the university".

Sam moved to the gate of the canteen and said, "You demon your death is near". Then he bowed his head and started thinking about his plan what he had. The electric shock that comes from the body of Sam, hit the iron rod and got distributed into many parts and struck all the men. Within seconds they all died.

All the people started clapping and they asked him his name. Sam did not know what to say. Then Sam told the people present in canteen, "I am ELECTROID". People started cheering for Electroid. Now he could not go out of the university walking because now he had became a super hero. Sam recalled that when he woke up, he was floating above the bed. As Sam thought of flying in the air, he rose and was into the air. That is when he understood that this powers worked by his thoughts. Sam flew and moved out of the University in a lofty speed. Exactly then, the last men of Dorgun attacked him in the air. Only Sam was given the power full electric punch l. Then men moved down to the land and there the land was rickety. Sam moved to his house and landed in his garden and took out the jacket and handkerchief and made his hair the way it normally was and moved inside the house and went to the bed to sleep.

In the morning, when he woke up he moved down. His mother July was watching the news. In the news the lady was saying that "A wee boy of approximately 18 years old showed courage and saved the University from the hijackers. But the people there tell us, that when he came there, the mobiles stopped working. His name was "Electroid". The bodies of the hijackers were sent for postmortem. And when the police removed all the bodies from out side the university were terrain was rickety, they saw a new type of a pattern. The scientist told that it was related to the meteor fallen in the Bellwood jungle 18 years back but there were no clues present. And also the lady of the news channel informed, "the bodies had gone for the postmortem and the bodies had disappeared before the procedure. The Electroid's news was also highlighted in the news paper.

Sam said "Mom I would be in the garage. Don't disturb me. I am going to complete my experiment and before I complete it, I do not want you to come in there". Sam moved to the garage and set the equipment.

Sam took out the blood from his finger and started the blood test. And moved to the laptop to see the result. The result showed that some particle which produces electricity was attach to the RBC.

Now Sam, from this shoulder took out the tissue muscle for the experiment and then he stitched the part back. Sam made some biological experiment with the tissue muscle and the results were shown on the laptop. Sam went near to his laptop for the result. He was shocked that his tissue muscles also contained an element producing electricity.

After further more experiment, Sam confirmed that his RBCs had the element which produced electricity. And when the RBC went to the graveyard for there dying the element attach to it moves to new RBC's by jumping. And the tissue, muscle which has the element producing electricity is fixed by bonding and don't jump or move from its place.

Then he went upstairs and took out his toy box and started finding a pair of specks which was develop by his father James Yard. And an ear ring which was given by his mom July Yard". He finally found the things he wanted. The specs was latest in its technology with night vision technology.

Sam opens the specks and wore it and also opened the ear ring and wore it and made his hair stylish and went to see in the mirror. After looking at himself in the mirror he put all his things back and turned back from Electroid to Sam. He felt proud of himself that he looked smart and handsome in that avatar.

Chapter Helping

❋ ❋ ❋

Sam wanted the super hero costume which would match with his gadgets. Sam took out some clothes of blue, violet, red, green, orange and yellow colour. And also took out his father's boots. Sam started sketching his costume. First he made the pant and attached it with the boots. And also made upper costume. And also made the wing to look like handsome super hero. It took him three hours to complete it.

At night Sam wore his costume with the gadgets then he went to the mirror and said "Now I am looking like a super hero and lets test my powers". Then he moved faster towards the window and jumped. Sam was flying high above like a high speed jet.

After flying for a distance of a mile, suddenly his peace was disturbed near the backyard of a shop. Sam moved towards the voice and when he reached there, he saw some people were tying to rob a girl. It was dark but Electroid could see all the things by his fancy technology specks.

It was dark and suddenly the

robbers saw a man nearing them in a hero costume. One of them asked "Go away, you man!". Then Sam rubbed his fingers and pointed it to their direction. The darkness has ceased to exist. They could see Electroid clearly. One of them asked, "Who are you". "Electroid the spark hero" said Electroid. "You cannot do anything to us. We will rob you and all you will be able to do is to run home and cry".

The robbers moved towards Electroid. Electroid moved forward and fired the electric shock. The shock went from his hand and struck the robbers present there. Robbers went for a little nap after receiving the low intensity of shock. "What's your name, you handsome hero?" asked by girl. "I just now said" said Electroid. "At that time you were in a foul mood. Now tell me your name again with a smile, please?" said the girl. "My Name is 'Electroid' the sparky hero and you beautiful lady you should be careful while walking at night. Bye!" said Electroid. Electroid carried the robbers to the police station and threw them into the jail. Electroid moved towards his home.

When he reached his place, Sam took out his clothes and gadgets and jumped onto the bed and sleept.

In the morning when Sam went down, he saw the girl he has rescued. She was in the news and was reporting, "A hero came and saved my life. He was strong and handsome. He said his name was 'Electroid. The sparky hero'. I wonder where you are, my hero!". Sam instantly smiled after watching the news. He changed the channel of news. Every news channel has the same news; about Electroid. And the girl was also in talking about him in every channel. She also said that she had made a portrait of Electroid, and wanted to show it to the citizens of Bellwood.

A rumour was spread the police that, Electroid would kill all the thieves and robbers if they did not surrender to the police. The rumour spread in the city like fire. Due to the fear of dying, all the robbers and thieves surrendered themselves, as they preferred going to jail rather than being killed.

Bellwood city was free of robbers

and thieves. And the people lived freely in the city because there was terror of the Electroid towards the robbers and thieves and the love towards the people.

One evening, Sam and his friends planned to go for dinner. When they reached there, they saw Electroid's posters every where they saw; like shops, banner, digital tv, newspaper, building, etc. One friend of Sam's, Danny said, "Look over there! Everywhere Electroid has been advertised. What a hero I must say! I salute him". "Let's go and eat. Salute when you meet the hero himself" said Sam. Sam was felling happy within himself. All the friends and Sam ate food and returned to their residents.

Chapter Mountain

❄ ❄ ❄

Sam and all his friends were chatting on a text group. They planned to go for a tour in the mountains near Bellwood after 2 days at 4:00 clock in the morning.

The Day came of the tour. Sam and his friends were ready to depart. Sam's friends John, Booker, Cyril, George, and Patrick were going for the tour in their BMW X 7 together. But Sam was ready to go with his Harley Davidson..

Dorgun all this while had been thinking about those powers. He himself wanted to go to the Earth and get the powers from that boy..

The boys were riding on the roads of the mountain and all they could see were Mahogany trees everywhere.. Sam was riding his Harley Davidson, when suddenly a voice struck his ear, "I want your power boy. Give them to me or I will kill you and take the powers from your body". This voice was repeatedly falling into his ear and he lot his control on the bike and fell off a cliff.

After three hours, Sam opened his eyes and found him self lying on a bed of old house made of Mahogany wood. Sam hurried and made his way to open the door. As he opened the door, he saw an old man entering the house. "I found you lying with your bike in the forest. You have got hurt on your hands and legs. Firstly you relax" said the old man. "My friends and I were were on the tour and were riding on the mountains" said Sam. "How did you fall from the road" asked the old man. "I got a very strange voice in my ear that he wanted my powers otherwise he would kill me and take the powers" told Sam.

"Eureka! That power which I was looking for when I was young. I worked under Dorgun. When I felt that he was going to do wrong with your powers, then I escaped from this team and settled down in this place where he could not find me. Now you should not be late. Come with me, we should run. I have repaired your bike and will show you the exit to the forest" said the old man. "I am hungry" said Sam. "You take this pone and eat" said the old man. Sam ate the pone and moved with his bike. Sam was sitting at the back.

They rode for three miles when a fire ball struck the floor of the forest. Sam and the old man saw that a man fir fire on his body came from the sky and he was in a kneeling down position. When he stood up, his body fire set the entire forest on fire. The old man clarified that it was his master Dorgun. "Dorgun why have you come here" asked the old man.

Dorgun started laughing and said "What a surprise! My right hand is opposing me. I should imprison you, Mandy". "No Dorgun. You can not take the power from the boy. Firstly you should fight with me" said Mandy (the old man). "Mandy you know my fury. I can kill you. You have only one chance, give me the boy and save your life and get away from my eyes" said Dorgun. Mandy moved down from bike. "You go towards the west direction. You will find the road" said Mandy to Sam. "Mandy there is fire everywhere, what I do" said Sam. "Use your power and destroy the trees in the west and go" told Mandy.

Sam pointed it hand in the West

ward direction and fired electricity. All the trees in his direction fell, paving way towards the road. Sam started his bike, and with full speed moved towards the road.

Dorgun was extremely furious that his right hand, Mandy was saving the boy's life. Dorgun run fast towards Mandy and pierced his nails in Mandy's neck and threw him away. Within few second Mandy died. "I will take the power after which the boy will be killed" said Dorgun.

Sam drives his Harley with full speed. When he crossed three miles, he saw the road. Then he started driving on the road of the mountain. After crossing five miles, he saw a BMW X 7 on the road. When he reached near the car, he saw that nobody was there. Just then he heard a voice, "Sam where are you" it was Cyril's voice. "Oh! Friends I am near the car come fast" said Sam. "Lets go up. That is Sam's voice from near the car" said Patrick. The five friends went near the car where Sam was near his car. He has hurt his hands and legs. Then they took out an energy drink (red bull) from car and gave it to Sam. Sam drank it and felt good. George said, "Sam you should not be driving the bike. Go in the car, I will take the bike to your house". All the other four friends agreed. Sam sat in the car. It was 3:00 in the noon. They all returned to Bellwood. And George also starts Harley and return back to Bellwood.

John asked, "Sam how did you fall down". "I don't know but I know that my focus on the bike was lost" said Sam. "You know we where looking for you for four hours." said Booker. "Yes, friends I know" said Sam. "Sam I have heard that this mountain forest is huge and one can get lost very easily. How did you find us" asked Patrick. "When I woke up, I saw that, my bike and I were lying on the floor of the forest. Then I stood up and started my bike and moved in the west direction and found the road. After moving on road I found you all" replied Sam.

Their talk went on till they reached Sam's house. George come near the car asked Sam to open the garage as it had a code.

Sam got off the car and went near the garage and entered the pin 6374 the garage gate opened and George parked Sam's Harley Davidson in the garage.

July heard the bike's sound. She came near the door and opened it. She saw Sam and his friends at the door. July saw how Sam was terribly hurt. She said, "Come inside my child you have got terribly hurt". Sam and his friend moved inside the house. He sat on the sofa. July said "George open that almirah and take out the first aid box". George took out the first aid box and handed it to July. July started bandaging Sam and asked him the reason of his wounds. "Aunty he was driving his Harley and suddenly his he got distracted by a bird and landed into a pit. We all started finding him but he didn't he couldn't be found everywhere. After four hours he came to us and told about what had happen" Said John.

"Sam you will not ride bike till your wound is healed" said July.

"Ok mom I understood." replied Sam.

"Now you all must go home. Your parents are waiting for you all and thank you for taking care of my child" said Juli.

All five friends left the house for their homes.

"Sam you must rest" said July.

"Yes mom" said Sam.

Chapter Sniper

❄ ❄ ❄

"Sniper" said Dorgun.

"Yes my lord why have you made me? (hisss)" asked Sniper.

"For a very important mission " told Dorgun.

"Lord, what is the mission (hisss)" asked Sniper.

"Look at this tech. Hologram. This is planet earth there where is a city called Bellwood. In this city, a boy has a power, which I need. You have to destroy the that city and that boy too and take the power from his body and get it to me" said Dorgun.

"It will be my pleasure to do it (hisss)" said Sniper.

"Sniper, you have the power that your poison can freeze the brain of the people living on that planet" said Dorgun.

"Ok my lord (hisss)" replied Sniper.

Sniper moved towards the planet named 'Earth'.

When Sniper reached the earth, he moved towards the Bellwood city.

People saw a fire ball coming near the park. The fireball struck the floor of the park.

The smoke coming from the fire ball made the people's vision opaque. When the visions of the people got clear, they saw an umber colored snake whose head was in the shape of a skull and the tail was in the shape of a pointed arrow.

"Where is your deity to protect your life, humans? (hisss)"said Sniper.

Sniper moves towards the human present in the park and threw his poison onto the bodies of human. They all froze at their place and could not move their bodies. A small boy come near him and said "he is a part of God, he is our hero, come Electroid and destroy this demon". Sniper with his tail raised the child up in the air. "Now call your hero (hisss)" said Sniper. The small boy started shouting repeatedly "where are you Electroid?".

The information was released by the police and within a minute, police surrounded the park and said "leave the child and surrender yourself to the police". Sniper threw his poison in the direction of the police. The police officers froze in their place.

The news reporter's helicopter started flying above the park. The news camera started focusing on the sniper's activities.

At the university the news cracked among all the students. They all gathered in the hall and the projector was arranged. The news channel started and everyone watched the news. The lady on the news channel said, "This evil snake has captured the little boy and is calling out to our hero Electroid. Where are you Electroid? Please safe us and that innocent child".

Suddenly Sniper attacked the helicopter with an arrow on his tail. The helicopter crashed on the floor of the street. The news was stopped in the channel which was live. "Electroid please help us" said the lady on the news channel.

Sam saw all the things on the channel and rushed towards the almirah and open it and took out his costume and ran to the toilet. He wear the costume and all the gadget and made his hair hair. Then he broke the window by a punch and started flying like an airship.

Electroid reached near the park and went down to the park. He stood on the floor. "Our hero Electroid has come to defeat you, demon" said small boy. Sniper became angry and threw the boy in the air. Electroid flew up in the air and caught the small boy and moved towards the ground and put him down and said "go little boy. You are brave". With rocket speed, Electroid moved towards Sniper and hit him with an electric power punch. Sniper went into the air an struck a building. "Marvel my power you son of bitch!" said Electroid. Sniper came forward and threw his poison toward Electroid but he save himself. Now Electroid put his hand forward and fired ultra electric shock towards the Sniper. When the shock struck Sniper, he moved backward and fell into pond. "Now what can you do? You will throw electricity towards me and I will become a good conductor of electricity and the entire living organisms in the pond will die after getting the lofty shock. Only I can make the people live again (hisss)"said Sniper.

"I am not listening to you" replied Electroid.

Electroid around and saw a lasso collar and pulls it up and threw it towards Sniper. Sniper ducked but his tail went inside the lasso collar. Then electroid pulled him towards himself then his tail was tight with knot. Electroid spun him in the air and threw him on a tree. When Sniper struck the tree, the tree went down with Sniper and rebound to it's original position throwing Sniper from the tree and went to the grass floor like a catapult. Sniper was losing all his energy by now.

Electroid pulls the sniper out and caught him by the hand and said, "How can you return their life? tell fast!". "When I will suck the wound from their body then only they can live again (hisss)" said Sniper. "Now you do it other wise I will make you like a hayrick" said Electroid.

Electroid moved towards the people who froze. One by one, Sniper suck the wounds from there bodies. The wound which Sniper was sucking it was working on his body and slowly-slowly his body was freezing. When he sucked the wound of the last man present in the park, this entire body froze. Then Electroid threw him up in the air and moved as fast as a bullet and hit the sniper's body with Electroid's electric punch and the body of Sniper was spread in small parts and blasted.

The people present in the park started making hilarity of exult.

"Whenever any evil spirits looks at my Bellwood city, I will destroy everyone of them" said Electroid. And again flew back to his University.

He reached the university toilet to change his getup and moved out with a bag containing Electroid gadgets and costume. And kept the bag in the almirah and moved towards the hall where all the students were present.

"Where were you Sam?" asked Cyril.

"I was in the toilet" replied Sam.

"You have too see Electroid winning against the demon which was destroying the human race by freezing them" said Cyril.

"Yes my friend, I saw a part of

the news. I had to urgently go to the washroom because of which I could not watch the news further" said Sam.

Dorgun watched everything happening on the planet earth with Sniper. Dorgun felt very angry after seeing it. "I will not leave you Electroid and now I will be fighting with you. Just wait for sometime. Have all the fun you want to have for later you might not have the liberty to" said Dorgun.

The morning Alarm rang Tee…. Tee...Tee…...Tee…. . Sam woke up and stopped the alarm. It was a Sunday. Sam brushed his teeth and took a bath.

And when he reached downstairs he saw a journal on the sofa. Sam pulled it up and saw that the Electroid news was in the front page. It was written 'Inborn with the power he is our juvenescent hero who saved millions of life from the demon attacking the Bellwood city'.

Sam found that it has become a fad to save the life of the people. He smiled after reading the journal.

"Sam are you up?" asked July.

"Yes mom. I am down stairs in the

drawing room" replied Sam.

"You know that today is Sunday you should do purge the garden of the leaves" asked July.

"Mom I know. You need not worry. I will clean the garden" replied Sam.

"Go now" said July.

Sam went out in the garden and used his power of electricity on the ground. The leaves and dust moved in the side by the electricity. Now Sam collected the leaf and dust from the corner of the garden and put them in a garbage bag and threw it in the dustbin.

And returned in the house. "Mom your work has been done" said Sam.

"How did you clean the garden so fast?" asked July.

"Mom the wind was blowing in the north direction. The dust and leaves moved in the north direction and was itself blown to the corner of the garden. I had to only pick it up and throw them it into the dustbin" replied Sam.

"Forget the dustbin. Come fast into the kitchen. I have made your favourite pancakes" said July.

Chapter First
attack of Dorgun

* * *

The mayor of Bellwood city arranged a party in which all the people where invited. This Party was a tribute to our hero Electroid for saving us from the demon attacking the city.

The Party arrangement start 3 days before 23rd May. The party included dinner and drinks. The news of this party was advertised everywhere.

"Sam, come down fast" said July.

"What happen mom?" replied Sam.

"Come down first" said July.

"I am coming" replied Sam.

Sam moves downstairs and moved towards the drawing room.

"Why you have called me?" asked Sam.

"See this newspaper" said July.

"What is there? Give me" asked Sam.

Sam took the newspaper from his mom and started reading. It was written that 'Your mayor has organized big party for the Bellwood city. This Party is to pay tribute your hero Electroid for saving us from the demons. Our respected Mayor himself requests Electroid to come for the party and grace it with his presence.

"Mom, Electroid will come in the party?" asked Sam.

"He is the hero of the million of people in Bellwood. And when he will come in the party, all the Bellwood citizens will be happy and joyous otherwise they will be upset and disheartened.

"I think that he should come in the party" said Sam.

Sam moved to the garage and started his Harley Davidson and opened the door and moved out to see the reaction of the people after the news.

Sam saw that the kids were existed to see Electroid in the party and even the adults were existed to see Electroid.

The Day of the party came. All the people were excited to go that night but some people where started planning to kill the mayor. They were the big wanted criminals that escaped from the jail in the past few days. They wanted to take revenge from mayor because he was the one who put them behind bars.

On the day of the party, everyone started gathering in the park. Sam and her mother July also reached the park. Some time later, a royal car came in. And a man came out of the car. He wore an expensive black suit and pant with a red bow tie above the white shirt. He was the mayor of Bellwood city. He confidently moved towards the stage.

"Hello to all the people gathered in the park. The party will start once our hero Electroid is here" said mayor. All the people started clapping listening to their mayor.

Sam had no idea that millions of people would gather there. "Mom I have a work in my garage I will be finishing it and then I will reach here" said Sam.

"Sam, Electroid is coming. First see him then go" said July. Sam thought that if he wouldn't go home, how would Electroid come to the party!

"No mom, I have set the timer." Said Sam.

"I know your projects and sci-fi experiment. You are becoming like your dad. Go now, fast" said July.

Sam moved out of the park and started his Harley and moved towards this home in full speed. Within minutes he reached his house and went in the garage and parked his bike and rushed towards his room upstairs. He took out his Electroid costume and gadgets from the wardrobe.

Sam wore his costume and gadgets and made his hair. He jumped from his window and flew towards the park with the speed of electricity.

"See everyone! Electroid has come" said a small girl.

All the people in the park started cheering for him. Electroid landed on the stage.

"Your hero has accepted our request and come to the party" said the mayor.

Electroid raised his hands up and started waving in the air to say hello to the people gather in the park.

The mayor handed him the mic to Electroid. "Electroid can you tell about your power to the people?" said mayor.

"My power comes from the people and their happiness" replied Sam.

"What a fabulous answer" said the mayor. The people started clapping.

The assistance of the mayor handed a champagne bottle to Electroid and asked him to open it..

Electroid shook the champagne bottle and the cork of the bottle moved up in the air by the pressure. Electroid poured champagne in the glass which the assistant was holding.

Mayor and Electroid cheered the glass. Suddenly Electroid's eyes fell on the front building. There he saw two to three men. One was pointing the gun towards the mayor and a second later, he shoot a bullet towards mayor. Electroid push the mayor from the stage. Suddenly all the music stopped. People started seeing what had happened. Then a bullet struck the stage light and it blasted.

Electroid moved towards the building and launched his electric shock towards two to three men and they all went for a little nap after the small shock.

Electroid caught hold of two to

three men and pulled them out and threw them on a carpet and rolled them into it. Mayor noticed that they were the most wanted criminals who wanted to kill him.

"Electroid is great. He saved my life and caught hold of the most wanted criminals" said the mayor. The people started cheering for Electroid.

"I promise to save the city from all the evil spirts" said Electroid. And flew from the park.

Sam returned home and changed his dress. Then he started his Harley and moves again to the park. When he reach there. His mother told him, "You took too much time to come. Electroid was here with us" said July.

"Really? Electroid was here in the park? I missed the chance to see him" replied Sam.

Sam felt happy that everyone would now go home happily as they had seen Electroid at the party.

In the morning, Sam read the newspaper. It said, 'how Electroid saved the life of the mayor from the most wanted criminals and promised to save us from evil spirits. Reading the newspaper, a smile grew on Sam's face.

"Sam, come in the kitchen. I have made pineapple pie" said July.

"Yes mom! coming to taste your yummy pie" said Sam.

On the other side Dorgun was planning to go on earth the next day. "You say people and their happiness is your power. Haa… haa.. I will destroy the people and finish you and their happiness said Dorgun".

When Sam opened his eyes on the next day and moves towards his window, he drew the curtains and saw that the weather was absolutely superb. Suddenly the sky became red as fire and it looked like sky was throwing fite. Sam was confused about what was going on. Rain started pouring. But it was surprising as the rain did not have the usual water droplets, rather it had fire. Yes, it rained of fire. It destroyed everything on its way.

This fire rain was not just above Bellwood city, but over the whole of America. The president had alerted the entire country that no one should come out of their houses till the rain has stopped.

In all the news channel, they showed that God was portraying His curse on the people. But Sam didn't believe this. He thought someone else was behind all this.

As Sam was looking out of his window and wondering the reason behind this, he suudenly saw lava stones falling. Lava destroyed all the tall buildings, sky towers, homes, etc in America. The president was worried out the people because thousands of people had died, hundreds of them were in the hospitals. President ordered that all the people must become underground for their safety. Everyone went in the basements of their buildings. Most of the buildings were old and could withstand the harshest storms. The entire city was interconnected from underground and need not worry about the schooling or the working people for days together

A voice came from the sky "were is your superhero Electroid" said Dorgun. All the people were surprise to hear this. The satellite camera focused on the man in the sky. “Sir we can fire our bombs. He is just one and we are so many.” said the Army general.

“Who is he calling” said President.

“Sir there is a superhero in Bellwood city who has saved the lives of the entire city.” said the President’s assistant, Mary.

“I can’t wait for him, activate the atomic bomb and launch it on him” said President.

The atomic bomb was activated and launched towards Dorgun. When it struck Dorgun, a kind of a blast should have occurred but Dorgun absorbed the bomb. “Nothing happen sir” said the army general.

“No blast? How it that possible?” said the President.

“Sir we can launch hydrogen bomb to it” said Marry. “Yes, you are right. General, launch the hydrogen bomb to it” said president.

The hydrogen bomb was activated and launched. This bomb struck and blasted too but it blasted a little away from Dorgun and the blast partial destroys many buildings.

"Now Electroid only can save us" said Marry.

"Yes" said the President.

Sam secretly moved out from the under ground safety place and rushed to his home. He wore the Electroid costume. And made a safety shield over his body of electricity which would protect him from the fire rain and lava stones. He moved with high speed. And saw Dorgun from 150 meter. He moved with double the speed and struck Dorgun with the power of full electric punch. The rain of fire and stone of lava stopped falling.

President saw that some one struck the man and the rain and stone stop falling when they zoom in from the satellite camera, they saw Electroid strike with a punch of electricity. After striking he moved back to the building and struck the building one by one and when he stopped, the President saw him penetrating through twenty one buildings.

"You have such a weak hero, Americans!" said Dorgun from sky.

Sam again woke up and moved

towards Dorgun and hit him with full speed. But in return he again got a punch with double the power and .

"What a bad attempt to kill me! Don't you know I am stronger than you?" said Dorgun from the sky.

Sam stood up and flew towards him and put his hand forward. High voltage electric current rose from Electroid's hand and hit Dorgun. Dorgun moved a little back.

"I am like a pinprick that will kill you, you demon" said Electroid.

"Haa….Haa….Such little current can do nothing to me" said Dorgun.

They both were above Washington city. President sent ships to fire on Dorgun and tanks, army forces, fighter planes etc. Everything started firing towards Dorgun. Dorgun was filling uncomfortable because everything was firing from all the side. Electroid moved and hit Dorgun with super electric shock punch. Dorgun moved down to the floor and hit the ground. A hole was made by Dorgun when he was stricken.

Dorgun flew in the sky again and

with his power he flew all the equipment of army and threw them all. Electroid moved to save all the ships and tanks and the army people. Electroid flew with electric current speed. It took only a macro second to keep all the army equipment in their places.

"What speed you have Electroid, you surprise me. So much speed used to help them but they couldn't even see it. Because you move very fast and people in the ships, tanks, and land tthought that they were in sky and when you move there they saw that they all are safe" said Dorgun .

"You don't know I can speed up my power and my flying ability" said Electroid .

Fighter planes started firing on Dorgun. After a while they all crashed because Dorgun spread fire on the planes.

Electroid moved backward from the plane.

Electroid moved backward to the land.

"Hey Mr. Hero you are scared of me. And go to hide in your mother pouch" said Dorgun.

"(Laughing) you are mad son of bitch" said Electroid.

Electroid moved towards Dorgun with his whole power and hit Dorgun. Within a second both were at the same place but after a second Dorgun moved upward with the speed of superman. Dorgun moved out of the atmosphere of planet earth.

Electroid followed him but when the hero of America reached the outer space he couldn't see Dorgun. He couldn't see because it was too dark and his hi-tec specks (night vision) could provide vision only till a range. This hi-tec specks would start working when is was night. When light hit his glass, the night vision mode got over automatically.

When he saw a sun, the big ball huger then the earth coming near him, his eyes become blinded. He could hear some big stones of lava passing from beside him but he could not do anything because he had become blind.

When the millions of stones struck the atmosphere and returned towards the big sun which was coming near earth. Electroid could understand that the stones was returning back.

And the million of stone returned back towards the sun and hit the sun.

Suddenly the sun started disappearing and Dorgun started appearing after the striking of the million of stones.

"How did this happen!" said Dorgun.

This voice got in the ear of Electroid and his blindness was over. He could see Dorgun .

A voice came "Dorgun you can't destroy this planet when Lily is with Electroid" said lily.

Again Dorgun fired his holistic lava on the planet earth. But at the atmospheres layer repelled it back to Dorgun. But Dorgun ducked and saved his life.

Then a beautiful girl started appearing.

When Electroid saw the girl. As he saw her, he initially thought that she had come for him. A song started ringing in his ear-

When I saw you
You blew my mind
Just like you
Nobody is kind
(Rap)
Yellow-white dress you are girl so pretty
You make my mind so tricky
You have come from heaven
Seeing you, many women die
You just glow like a sun
Let's go and do some fun
I am single
Let's mingle
Singing Harshit in the air
Outer space love story started from here

(Rap ends)
Your bold figure
Deity given you this figure
I have fallen in love
Just like you pretty dove
Ouaa….. Ouaa……. Ouaa….. lalala
…..lalala……. lalala….

Song ends.

Electroid was staring Lily and

became a statue. Dorgun saw that this human hero had fallen in the love and just then he fired lava towards Electroid. Suddenly Lily moved fast and picked Electroid (which became statue after seeing lily) in her arms and moved to a distance when that Lily said "Sam are you hearing me. Let's finish this Dorgun first". Electroid again come into the real life from love life.

Both Electroid and Lily fired their special attack towards Dorgun.

When it struck Dorgun, he was not able to fight after his special attack of Lily and Electroid .

"I will come again" said Dorgun.

Dorgun moved from there by saying the line.

"I will come again at the right time and let you know everything Sam" said Lily.

Suddenly Lily started disappearing.

Electroid moved towards the earth and saw that all the people of America had gathered on the road and started cheering Electroid to safe them.

Chapter Pet

* * *

The roads, building, sky towers were completely repaired in 10 days. America was back on it's foot with his beauty.

The President also agreed Electroid as the shield of America.

Dorgun was orbiting around the earth because he had lost from the humans and had become very weak. "I will send alien to earth. That would seem to be pet and people will start loving him. This love towards the pet will destroy all the things in America" said Dorgun .

One night, a mother and her daughter were strolling at night.

"Mom, see, something gleamed"

"It's a pet girl" tempted.

"I want to get one"

"No" said mom.

"See, that poor pet is shuddering".

Mom made herself clear by saying a no again.

The small girl started wailing.

Mom said "you can take it" finally.

"You will have to take care of him" Mom clearing out.

Small girl took that pet and took

to there home with a big smile at her face. She named the pet "Guffi". Guffi was a loving pet.

Sam went out in the park for a walk. July was cleaning the house. When she moved to Sam's room. She was cleaning his wardrobe. What she saw was amazing. Sam had the costume of Electroid. She thinks that Electroid might be Sam. When there is a problem comes Sam always goes out secretly. Like during the party hosted by the Mayor, he said that he had to complete his work. The moment he left, Electroid emerged. And when Electroid leaves, Sam returns. The second clue was when everyone went underground. Even then Sam had disappeared. Both these clues, with the third of seeing the costume, made July confirm that he was the America's superhero Electroid which millions of people praise her son and give him their blessings .

"Mom I have come back" said Sam.

"Come upstairs Sam" said July.

Sam moved towards his room.

"What happen mom?" said Sam.

"My son is the current generation machine" said July.

"What mom you are saying?" asked Sam.

"I have found Electroid's costume. It is the same size as of you and gadgets given by your dad. I am certain that you are Electroid" said July.

"Yes mom you are right. I am the current machine of America" said Sam.

"Why did you tell to your mother?' asked Juli.

"I thought of telling you earlier but did not get the time and opportunity to" said Sam.

"I love you my hero, Electroid" said July.

"I love you too mom" said Sam.

July kissed her son Sam on his cheeks and huged him.

"You are only the virtually my hero" said July.

"Thanks mom" replied Sam.

Phone rang and Sam received it. It was George on the other side.

"Hello, Sam?" said George.

"Yes George, what happen?"

replied Sam.

"Bellwood city vs Washington DC, for football match" said George.

"Who all are selected?" said Sam.

"Cyril, you, Me, John, Patrick, Booker, Howard and Markus are selected" Said George .

"When is the match and were is it being held?" asked Sam.

"Its day after tomorrow in Washington ground of football held by American football association. You should be ready tomorrow at 11:00 am. Bus will pick you from your home" said George.

"No practice at all?" said Sam.

"Have you forgotten we are champions?" said George.

"Bye. See you tomorrow" said Sam.

"Bye" replied George. And cut the phone.

"What Happen Sam?" asked July.

"Mom I have a football match tomorrow. The bus is coming to pick me from here. I have to pack up the thing" replied Sam.

"Who are you playing against?"

asked July.

"Washington DC" said Sam.

Next day Sam was ready to go. Bus was on time to pick him up.

They all reached Washington at 8:00 pm and reached the hotel and had their meal and went to their rooms, which were allotted to them and slept.

The match was at the morning 9:00 clock. All the boys were ready with their clothes and took the bus and reached the football stadium.

Many people had gathered at the stadium for the match.

"Five times in a row champions, Bellwood city team has just arrived onto the stadium. Also, our three times champions have, Washington team is here" said the anchor.

Clapping and cheering was accompanied by the people.

"Bellwood team has George as their captain, Howard, the goal keeper, Sam, Cyril, Marcus, John, Patrick, Booker. And Washington team has Smith as their captain, Robert the goal keeper and Frank, Troy, Joseph, William, Joe, Warner" said the anchor .

"Both the team come to the ground for the national anthem" said the refry.

The national anthem started and finished within a minute.

"Captains, come forward for the toss" said refry .

George and Smith come forward.

"George what you will take? Heads or Tails?" asked refry.

"Heads" said George.

The coin was tossed and it fell on the ground. It was head.

"Which side of the ground you will take George?" asked the Refry.

"Right side" said George.

The boys took their positions on the ground and the whistle for the match to begin rang.

While the match was going on, the small girl gave Guffi food to eat. She gave him the food to eat. Each time Guffi ate, his size grew a little more. The small girl made Guffi walk outside. She did not use the collar and started talking with his friend and where ever Guffi went, he ate something non bio degradable. And every time he ate, he rapidly increased in weight and height. When the Small girl searched for Guffi, she saw a large four floored huge animal destroying the buildings. The little girl got terrorized by the huge creature and ran to her mother and hugged her.

"What happen my child?" said the mother of small girl.

"There is a huge animal outside" said small girl.

The little girl's mother saw out side through the window and saw that she was saying truth. Both of them ducked down.

Guffi slowly destroyed all the buildings. And eat dustbins, building, raw material and increased his weight and height. From four floored he became big as huge as eight floors wild animal. By running he reached the football stadium and entered it by breaking it and started eating the broken material. Before the Guffi entered the stadium the score was 0-0 and the half time had completed and the boys gone for the rest off the ground.

When all the people saw Guffi they moved out of the stadium to save their lives. Sam saw that huge wild animal he knows her mother July had kept Electroid costume in his bag. Sam rushed to the dressing room and changed the costume and move out. When he came out of the room to the ground. He pulled Guffi up in the air and threw him in the sea. Electroid was going to give him a punch of Electroid then a voice came "please my hero don't do this. He is my pet Guffi" said a small girl. Electroid stopped and when he turned back and saw small girl suddenly a big pink tongue comes and picked him in the air and threwn him away. Electroid fell on the ground. Guffi's legs were going to crush. Electroid felt a hand under his legs which caught hold of him and threw Guffi into the sea again. Electroid saw that Lily had again helped him.

"Electroid are you all right?" said Lily.

"Yes my dear" replied Electroid.

"We can not kill, but my magic can separate the evil spirit from the dog and the real Guffi will be separated" said Lily.

"Then do it" replied Electroid.

Lily moved her hand front and

started saying a few words. Guffi moved up in the air in a Yellow colour strong ball. A white light flash occured. Electroid and Lily saw that the small Guffi was there and the big evil was speaking from him. After the real Guffi fell down, Electroid caught hold of it and took the pet to the small girl. "Take your sweet dog. Oh! Sorry your sweet Guffi" said Electroid.

"Thank you my hero" replied the small girl.

Lily threw the yellow ball with the evil spirit in the air. Electroid with his electric power punch moves towards the ball and penetrated the ball with his power. And the evil spirit blasted in the air.

"First finish your match" said Lily."Ok" said Electroid.

Electroid secretly went and changed his dress and came to the ground. The match started again with the with the full spirit of game.

The last 10 second were left. Sam had the ball. He moved to the goal post and gave his best efforts and kicked the ball. But the goal keeper could not save the goal and Bellwood won and became the champions for the sixth time of the America association of football.

There was a celebration party for winning the match. After the party, everyone left for their homes. Just while Sam was leaving, he felt a hand grab his hands and pull him.

"Why you have pull me" said Sam.

"I am Lily, come with me" said Lily.

Some time later as Lily explains, she tells him, "Quarters of the sun's power is with you, me and Dorgun" said Lily.

"Where are you taking me?" asked Sam.

"Don't question" replied Lily.

Lily by her magic opened a teleporter and both of them moved inside.

"Which place is this?" asked Sam.

"Amazon jungle" replied Lily.

"Why have you brought me here?" asked Sam.

"Sam I had to tell you the reality of your life and in this place Dorgun can not search u. He will find you in America not in the Amazon jungle" replied Lily.

"What is my reality, tell me Lily"

asked Sam.

"I was just two years old when my planet blasted. My father sent me in a space craft. When your father activities the meteor in the form of sparky ball. That meteor was a part of my father which had the power of a King. My father had cursed Dorgun and said when my part I will absorbed, only then you would be free from my curse. And my father didn't know that it will come to this planet and Sam your father had the ability to activate it. My father thought it would be far and far away in the universe" said Lily.

"I was just three years old than my father had died in this lab" said Sam.

"You don't know that your father had activated the sparky ball when Dorgun was left from curse. And when he saw more power like him, he thought to absorb it and rule this universe. Your father saw that a man from sky was coming to his lab and he took the sparky ball and opened his handmade teleporter and reached you and the power was absorb by you when you were sleeping. And he returned back to his lab and Dorgun came in his lab and asked for the power ball but your father didn't replie him. So Dorgun killed him and everyone thought it was accident" said Lily.

"How did you know all the things and what else do you know about me" said Sam.

"I was in my space craft and saw Dorgun move towards earth. From that time I started tracing you. When you were 18 years old and he done a mistake in your project, and got a shock and you thought you had died but when your eyes opened, you were on the bed. That night I came to your house and used my magic and lifted you to your bed because I wanted to show you the power of yours to search more about it. Firstly the activated power news came to me then it went to Dorgun" said Lily.

"Tell me about your life" said Sam.

"My Life was spent in a space craft. But my father had left tech. Hologram. I could see what was happening and what had happened in the past" said Lily.

"From which age were you on the space craft?" asked Sam.

"From two years old to eighteen years and know I am with you" replied Lily.

"Tell me about your planet" asked Sam.

"My planet is Star neo which was the beautiful, peaceful, and a magical planet. All the people were living peacefully there. My father Alberton, was the king of that beautiful planet. King lit up the planet with his magic. Only this planet has neither fight before with any one" replied Lily.

"I want to know more about your planet Starneo" asked Sam.

"When I was born in Starneo all the people of that planet started celebrating that a princess is born. And all the people saw my bright face and started calling me Lily our princess. All the things was going right and then something happened that put our lives in danger" said Lily.

"Tell me, what was that danger?" asked Sam.

"The danger was Locto and his 3 millions of army men. They all go and destroy the different species in the universe. Now they want to destroy the beautiful planet Starneo. My father called Morono and said 'Morono you are the general of this planet and I want you to be leading the army of Starneo because I want to spend my time with my daughter Lily' and Morono says that 'You spend your time with your daughter and I will destroy the Locto and his army'. The people of my planet were ready to fight with the Locto army and wore their suits for the fight in the sky" said Lily.

"What happen in the fight?" asked Sam.

"Morono the general commanded the army and attacked Locto army. Our Starneo army were about 50 thousands people and the Locto army had double the men in our army. The Locto army had the power of muscles and our army has the power of magic. The fight started. Both the armies were fighting among them. But Morono used his magic of fire and in one second he destroyed out one million of people of Locto. Locto felt exasperated and used his power of muscle and destroyed forty thousands people of Starneo. Only ten thousands people were left in the army of Starneo planet. My father saw all this it and activated the Starneo super blaster and fired it to the army of Locto and the whole army was destroyed only Locto was left there" said Lily.

"What happen with Locto? Tell me Lily." asked Lily.

"Then Locto and Morono were there in the battle sky field and Morono said 'go back to the army of Starneo. To your homes. I will come after destroying this demon'. All the army of Starneo went back to their homes. Locto and Morono were present. Morono use his body and covered Locto in the flame of lava and Locto could not do nothing. He was tried and could not fight with Morono and he doubled his power of lava flame and destroyed Locto. After destroying Locto, Morono saw a black gem flying in the sky and he caught hold of that gem and kept it with him" said Lily.

"What happened next?" asked Sam.

"Sam, next all the people of Starneo started celebrating our win against

Locto. My father awarded the flame stone which Morono had absorbed after getting it. And the magic stone had touched my chest and my body absorb that power" replied Lily.

"What a queer planet it was" said Sam.

"Not strange it was. It was cleaner and healthier than your planet earth" said Lily.

"Lily my word made you angry. I'm sorry for that" said Sam.

"No, I'm not angry" said Lily.

"Tell me your beautiful moments spent on your planet Starneo" asked Sam.

"I was 2 years old my father Alberton made me sit on his shoulder and showed me whole planet and told me what is right and what is bad. In those days I felt like a princess. When people saw their king carrying his daughter on his shoulder, they said to my father that we will take our princess. Why you are doing our king? He laughs and says to the people that my little girl doesn't go to any body else only me and his mother and Morono. And all the people gave lots of gifts to me" said Lily.

"What a life Lily" said Sam.

"Sam, your life was better then me" said Lily.

"How?" said Sam.

"My life was spent in a space craft and was spent in tracking you.. Your life was spent with your mother and friends and you had fun with them" said Lily.

"Don't be Lily" said Sam.

"Yaa you are right why should cry know my aim is to kill Dorgun and free your planet from that demon. So that your planet's people can live freely and not blast like my planet because of some demon present there" said Lily.

"No Lily there is only one demon who is Dorgun. There are not many" said Sam.

Sam moved forward and wiped the tears of Lily and held her face and kissed her on the lips for a while.

"And somebody cheated on our planet starneo" said lily.

"Who cheated on your planet?" asked Sam.

"Morono" replied Lily.

"What happen over there? Can you explain?" asked Sam.

"The full moon became half. The sky became black and that happen..."said Lily.

"Tell me Lily, what happen?" asked Sam.

"The black gem got by Morono and he just broke it. The black spirit started entering his body. My father used his magic and saw that the people's soul were going into Morono's body. This outraged my father and he moved to my room and woke me up and told me to come with him. He then moved to to my mother's room. But he was too late. Her spirit was going from her body to the place where black magic goes. Where the black magic goes, that place always becomes black. Father held me up and started running to the room where the space craft was kept. And started the space craft and moved from that planet to the space" said Lily.

"How did your planet blast?" asked Sam.

"My Father and I could see from outside the space craft that our beautifully coloured planet started becoming black. And it became so black that my Starneo blasted like an exposed bomb. We were able to see the parts of our soil, buildings and the people around us. Suddenly all the parts started moving backward to their place. We could see Morono absorbing the parts in his body. When he absorbed the parts my father left me in the space craft and moved towards the Morono and said 'Why are you doing this?'. 'I am not Morono I am Dorgun' replied Dorgun. My father gave him a curse by using this power and said 'When my part will be not activated you will be not able to release your self from your dreams'. After saying this, he used his powesr towards Dorgun and Dorgun went to sleep. My father then converted into a meteor. He thought that no one moved in the universe. And the universe would be free from the black spirits and Dorgun too. And when I was 5 years old, your father had activated the meteor in the form of sparky ball and Dorgun again woke up" said Lily.

"What a sad story" said Sam.

"I started loving you Sam" said

Lily.

"Would you like to become my girl friend?" said Sam.

"Yes, my boy friend!" replied Lily.

Again they kissed each other for a while but this time Lily did it.

"My mom will be waiting for me" said Sam.

"Have you told anyone that you are Electroid? " asked Lily.

"Only my mom" replied Sam.

"Then I can live with you" said Lily.

"Why not, sure" said Sam.

Lily moved her hand forward and started saying the magic words. Suddenly the teleporter opened to his house. They both entered it and reached Sam's garden. Both of them moved to the front door and rang the bell. July opened the door and said "Where were you and who is she?". "Mom first let's go inside the house, then I will tell you the entire story" said Sam. All the three moved inside the house and went to the living room. Sam sat on the sofa and said "She is Lily, my girlfriend. She has come from Starneo planet". And told the story to her mom. "My husband was killed by that Dorgun who wanted to destroy America and the whole world" said July.

"Yes" said Lily.

In the meanwhile:

Dorgun was making plans to attack America and destroy the planet earth.

"I am coming Electroid be ready for your death" said Dorgun.

Electroid and Lily went to the white house to meet the President. When they reached there, they saw he was in some meeting. A person was at the door, he went inside and said "sir Electroid and a super girl want to meet you".

President left all his work and came out of the conference room.

"What happen my hero?" asked the President.

"I want to make a request" said Electroid.

"What is the request?" said the President.

"All the people of America should go underground again" said Electroid.

"Why?" asked the President.

"Dorgun can attack us again with his double power" told Lily.

"General, tell everyone to go underground as soon as possible" said President.

All the people of America were safely underground within an hour.

"Any more help Electroid?" asked President .

"All the defense need to fight Dorgun" replied Lily.

"Your work will be done" said President.

All the army forces are ready to fight. And the people were safely underground. All the missiles, bombs, atomic and hydrogen bomb, aircraft, submarines, battle ships were activated and were at their position to attack the army of Dorgun. They knew that Dorgun would come again with his army because Lily could feel more black spirits in Dorgun.

Chapter
Last War

* * *

Belligerent army of Dorgun were planning to attack America by entering the atmosphere of earth.

Electroid used this power and made an invisible shield of electricity the atmosphere of earth. Army, tanks, ships, fighter planet were set to attack the army of Dorgun.

"President I want to make America look hazy from above" said Electroid .

"General, use smoke machine from all the places and corners of America and make America look hazy" said President.

All the smoke machines was activated. After an hour, whole of America was covered under the smoke. Electroid's plan was, that when Dorgun's army would enter the atmosphere, they would then see that America would be under smoke and they wouldn't be able to fire. And suddenly our army would fire rapidly then there will be no area to go for Dorgun army until they are dead.

Electroid and Lily thought the

plan to work out. Electroid and Lily moved up in the air and waited for the army to come.

Dorgun and his army crossed the atmosphere of earth and then Dorgun said "attack". Except him, all the army crossed the invisible Electroid shield. Dorgun's plan worked on his army because when they crossed the sheild they got very high shock and they died.

"Wait!" said Dorgun. Only one third of the army was destroy and rest of them were safe. Dorgun moved his hand forward and fired the lava stone and when the lava stone struck the shield, it made a hole in it and Dorgun shouted, "Move in fast". All the army and Dorgun moved inside and suddenly the shield repaired itself and Dorgun's one forth army was destroyed.

After entering the earth, Dorgun came in front of Sam. Dorgun was confused about were people go, suddenly firing started from hazy America. Dorgun's army could not fire because they were not able to see them. For a second, the firing stopped. The firing was very severe and maximum army of Dorgun was destroyed. Only ten thousand demons were left in Dorgun's army.

Dorgun used his power and thought he could remove the smoke but Electroid gave him a punch. Dorgun moves down in the sea. Lily used her magic and destroy two thousand demons in a second. Suddenly, Dorgun recovered all his powers and attacked Electroid. When he struck Electrode, Electroid moved upwards but Dorgun moved very fast and hit Electroid on his chest and Electroid moved down wards and penetrated through thirty buildings. Firing again started, the fighter plane attacked his army, the atomic and the hydrogen bomb were launched together on the army. But all the fighter planes were destroyed by Dorgun with the power of flame. When atomic and hydrogen bomb collided with each other, it killed the entire Dorgun's army. And this full exploring making Dorgun fall again in the sea and Lily used her magic and covered her self and saved her self from that powerful explosion and Electroid made an electric sheild and saved the army people from the force explosion.

Dorgun moved upward in the air. And suddenly Electroid came with full speed with his powerful electric attack. Dorgun caught hold of the electric in his hand and rotated him in the air and threw him. When Electroid was falling down, suddenly he got fixed in the air and his power moved from his body and got absorbed by Dorgun. Dorgun used his black magic t absorb his powers. When the power was absorbed by Dorgun, Electroid fell down on the ground of America. When the army saw that their hero was losing, they again started firing "you all are frivolous" cried Dorgun.

Dorgun used his power and moved the sea water onto the land. It came like a Tsunami and all the buildings were under the water. But nothing could harm the people, as they were safely underground.

Lily picked Electroid from the sea water and took him to the hospital building.

"Where is your hero? tell me? I have absorbed his power now he cannot do anything" cried Dorgun.

He opened his hand and all the army equipments which were floating and the world's electricity started to get absorbed by Dorgun.

All the people under ground were afraid that their hero was losing his powers. They worried about who would fight with the demon now! They started praying to God.

When Electroid's eyes opened. The first thing he saw was Lily in front of him. He was sleeping on the bed of a hospital.

"Dorgun said that he had absorbed your power. Can you test your power Electrode?" said Lily.

"Yes sure" said Electroid.

Electroid moved two fingers closer, rub them and then pointed them to a distance. To his surprise, there was no electricity being produced.

Electroid into the blood test lab of hospital. He took his blood from his finger in a glass slide and started the blood test. He went to a computer to see the result. The result showed that the element that produced electricity was no longer present or attached to the RBC.

"What happen Electroid?" asked Lily.

"I can not fight with Dorgun anymore because I don't have the power left" replied Electroid.

"I don't think so" said Lily.

The prayers of many people convinced God to give Electroid another chance of testing his tissue muscles.

Electroid scrapped out little tissue from his shoulder and started experimenting on it. The result showed that only party of his power had gone, not entirely. His tissue still had the element producing electricity attached with the high bond between tissue muscle and the element producing electricity .

After many experiment, Electroid concluded that the element producing electricity on RBC was not attached with a strong bond. And the tissue muscle was attach with the element producing electricity was attach with very strong bond.

"Lily, see my tissue has the element producing electricity" said Electroid.

"Oh! Great" said Lily.

"That day I got an electric shock then the RBC attach elements were activated. Now I need severe electricity. Then the tissue one will get activate" said Electroid.

Both of them reached the transformer area upstairs. Electroid moved the wire out from the transformer with both the ends and held the wire In both the hands. Electroid got such a severe shock that all the electricity was absorbed by him and the electricity which Dorgun was absorbing from the world was also absorbed by Electroid. Dorgun felt confused about what was going on. (Dorgun was absorbing Bellwood's electricity. On the other hand he was absorbing world's electricity and when Electroid absorbed the Bellwood's electricity, then Dorgun became a good conductor of electricity and through him Electroid absorbed the electricity of the world). In the world all the lights, fans, and electric equipment stopped working.

After absorbing Electroid fell onto his knees. Lily moved to pick him but

Electroid shown his hand to stop.

"Lily now I can feel the power at the maximum peak. You use your magic to remove this water from America" said Electroid.

Electroid penetrated through the hospital building very fast which could not be calculated in second. And faced Dorgun.

Lily used her power and remove the water from America. And the water returned back to the sea.

"What a surprise! How did you get your power back?" asked Dorgun.

"The love of the people let me come back with my power. The old power was just the trailer and now I will show you full movie of my power" told Electroid.

Dorgun fired his flame towards Electroid but Electroid ducked him self and gave Dorgun a powerful punch in his full speed and Dorgun moved up in the air and struck the invisible electric shield and got shock that made an invisible electric shield break. The Sheild was over. And Dorgun stopped at the middle and again stood up with his power.

Suddenly Electroid used his full power towards Dorgun. And Dorgun was covered with mighty shock and after a second a black spirit left Morono and went up in the air and destroyed by getting very high shock which was the power shock of Electroid .

And Electroid used his power and fell down on the ground. He was not alive. Super hero had gone into deep sleep.

Chapter
Return of hero

❄ ❄ ❄

The super hero went to the deep sleep. Lily ran towards Electroid's body. All the people moved from under ground safety place and reached the body of Electroid. They started praying for the Return of the hero. The death of Electroid made people surprise and they all thought that earth had stopped orbiting around the Sun. Lily was crying on the body of Electroid .

When Morono's eyes opened he saw that all the people were gathered to see something. Morono was confused about where he was. And flies over the sky and Seeing a girl crying on the body of someone, he slowly moved down towards Lily. When he saw the locket in Lily's neck Morono said "What happen my princess? why are you crying on his body".

"He is only the man who had freed you from our rivals. And now he died" said Lily.

"I just know that I had broken the black gem accidently. Ever since then I was under the influence of black magic?" asked Morono.

"Yes Morono, now you our alive

and my true love has died" replied Lily.

"And where is our planet and what happen to our king?" asked Morono.

"That planet has blasted by that black spirit and our people have died in saving their planet" replied Lily.

"(Smiling) Princess, I don't have the power to give him life again but you have" said Morono.

"Are you joking" said Lily.

"No princess, you have the locket in your neck which has the golden juice of life from the tree that was was disappearing in Starneo. Your father had made a locket and put the juice in it. Break that locket and pour the juice on his body. Then he will be alive" replied Morono.

Lily broken the locket and poured the juice on Electroid's body. After a second, Electroid was returning to his real life and when his eyes opens then Lily kissed Electroid.

The End

Electroid 2 : The run off

HIV is coming soon

About my self

❄ ❄ ❄

I am Harshit Agrawal. I was born on 23 May 2000 in Mubarakpur, Azamghah. I am a budding author. I started writing my book when I was in class 11 in the hostel of Daffodils Public School, Mirzapur. I have written many poems in English and Hindi too. Some poems are on nature, disability, true first love, maa, etc. Electroid is my first book and the second part of Electroid would be Electroid 2: The run off HIV. I was only 16 when I started writing my first book.